P9-COO-901

THE NIGHT BEFORE CHRISTMAS

By Clement C. Moore
Illustrated by Corinne Malvern

A GOLDEN BOOK • NEW YORK

Copyright © 1949, copyright renewed 1976 by Random House, Inc. All rights reserved. Published in the United States by Golden Books, an imprint of Random House Children's Books, a division of Random House, Inc., 1745 Broadway, New York, NY 10019. Originally published in slightly different form in the United States by Golden Press, Inc., New York, in 1949. Golden Books, A Golden Book, A Little Golden Book, the G colophon, and the distinctive gold spine are registered trademarks of Random House, Inc. A Little Golden Book Classic is a trademark of Random House, Inc.

Educators and librarians, for a variety of teaching tools,
visit us at
www.randomhouse.com/teachers
Library of Congress Control Number: 2010934722
ISBN: 978-0-375-86359-2
Printed in the United States of America
10 9 8 7 6 5 4 3 2 1

Random House Children's Books supports the First Amendment and celebrates the right to read.

'Twas the night before Christmas when all
through the house
Not a creature was stirring, not even a mouse.

The stockings were hung by the chimney with care,
In hopes that Saint Nicholas soon would be there.

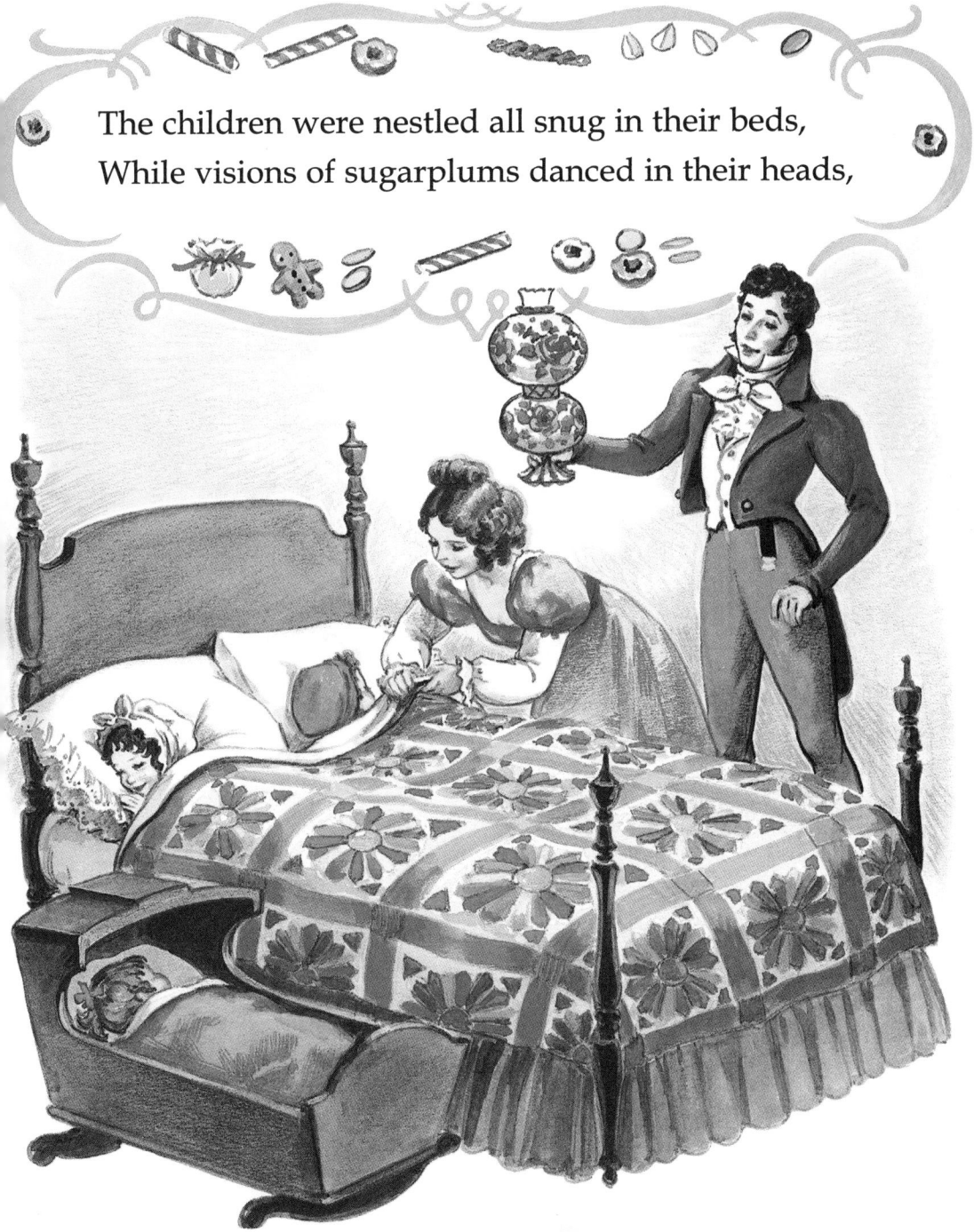

The children were nestled all snug in their beds,
While visions of sugarplums danced in their heads,

And Mama in her kerchief and I in my cap
Had just settled down for a long winter's nap
When out on the lawn there arose such a clatter,

I sprang from my bed to see what was the matter.
Away to the window I flew like a flash,
Tore open the shutters and threw up the sash.

The moon on the breast of the new-fallen snow
Gave a luster of midday to objects below,
When, what to my wondering eyes should appear,
But a miniature sleigh, and eight tiny reindeer;

With a little old driver, so lively and quick,
I knew in a moment it must be St. Nick.

More rapid than eagles his coursers they came.
And he whistled, and shouted, and called them
by name:
"Now, Dasher! now, Dancer! now, Prancer!
and Vixen!
On, Comet! on, Cupid! on, Donder and Blitzen!
To the top of the porch, to the top of the wall!
Now, dash away, dash away, dash away all!"

As dry leaves that before the wild hurricane fly,
When they meet with an obstacle, mount to the sky,

So up to the house-top the coursers they flew
With a sleigh full of toys, and St. Nicholas, too.

And then in a twinkle, I heard on the roof
The prancing and pawing of each little hoof.
As I drew in my head, and was turning around,
Down the chimney St. Nicholas came with a bound.

He was dressed all in fur, from his head to his foot,
And his clothes were all tarnished with ashes and soot;
A bundle of toys he had flung on his back,
And he looked like a peddler just opening his pack.

His eyes, how they twinkled! his dimples, how merry!
His cheeks were like roses, his nose like a cherry.
His droll little mouth was drawn up like a bow,
And the beard on his chin was as white as the snow.

The stump of a pipe he held tight in his teeth,
And the smoke, it encircled his head like a wreath.
He had a broad face and a little round belly
That shook, when he laughed, like a bowl full of jelly.

He was chubby and plump, a right jolly old elf.
And I laughed when I saw him, in spite of myself.

A wink of his eye, and a twist of his head
Soon gave me to know I had nothing to dread;

He spoke not a word, but went straight to his work,
And filled all the stockings; then turned with a jerk,

And laying his finger aside of his nose,
And giving a nod, up the chimney he rose.

He sprang to his sleigh, to his team gave a whistle,
And away they all flew like the down on a thistle.

But I heard him exclaim as he drove out of sight,

"Happy Christmas to all and to all a good night!"